Destiny is Mine!

WRITTEN BY DR. TERRY J. FLOWERS

ILLUSTRATED BY J.C. WALTER

Inspired Forever Books
Dallas, Texas
(888) 403-2727
https://inspiredforeverbooks.com
"Words with Lasting Impact"

Library of Congress Control Number: 2022909290
Paperback ISBN 13: 978-1-948903-66-0
Printed in the United States of America

To the Glory of God, this book is dedicated to the memory of Ethel Jackson, Juanita Branch, Gwendolyn Barjon, Gonzalo Say and to the multitude of faculty, staff, volunteers, and supporters of St. Philip's School and Community Center.
Their compassionate commitment to education enables the St. Philip's Creed to resonate within the lives of countless children for generations to come.

Look at me.
I am more than what you see.
Destiny is mine!
If it is to be, it's up to me.

2

3

Society will condemn,
but only I determine my path.

My people have suffered and died
for my chance to read and do math.

Just as sacrifices were made
to make my future bright,

it is my responsibility
to do things that are right.

I must start today to pave the way.
The community and the world
need my contributions.
In success, I will not stray.

The bias, the rumors,
nor the stereotypes will hinder my growth;
I claim dignity and prosperity.
My God promises both.

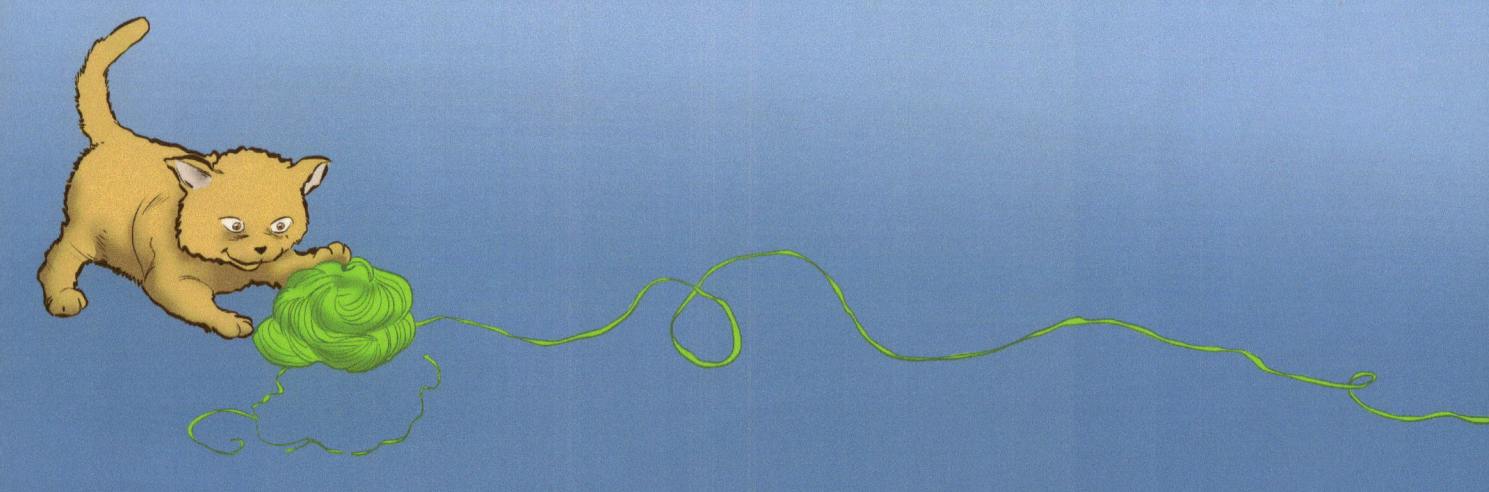

11

Look at me!
I am sharp, empowered, talented
and proud without limit.

I will use my education
to explore new heights.
The sky is the limit,
if I just put my mind in it.

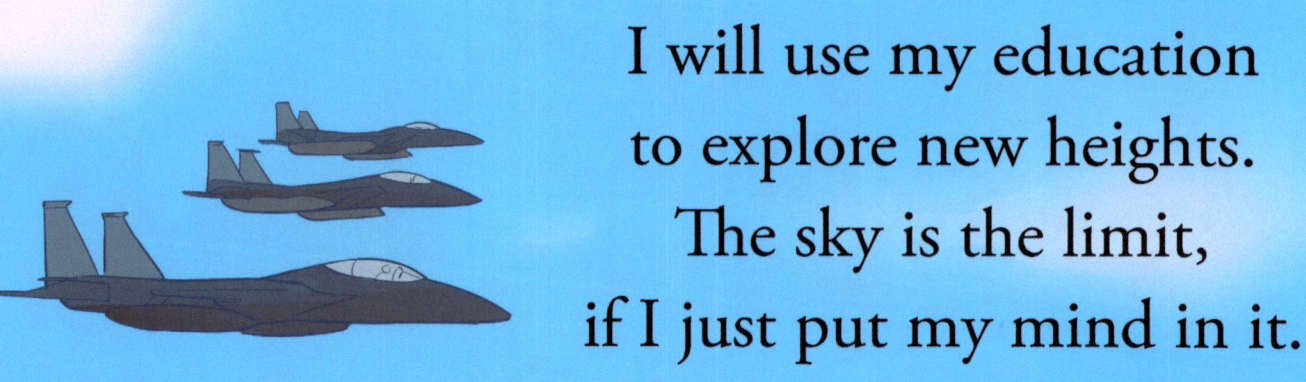

When I say, "stick it out,"
I don't mean a hand.

I will persevere to play my role
in God's omniscient plan.

I will live by "put ups, not put downs"
for my sister and my brother.

I care for you; I respect you.
If I don't, why should another?

Success is my right - failure my option.
I have the voice.
The consequences I will accept,
for I made the choice.

Look at me!
Great things lie ahead.

Judge me not by what you've been told,
but by what's in my head.

25

Dr. Terry J. Flowers serves as The Perot Family Headmaster of St. Philip's School and Community Center, where he started in service as principal in 1983. Dr. Flowers grew up on Chicago's South Side, ultimately finding a calling to work with young children. The titles of his three master's degrees attest to his commitment to education: Early Childhood Education (University of Northern Iowa), Curriculum and Instruction and Educational Administration (Columbia University). He also completed a doctorate in Education at the Teacher's College of Columbia University in 1995.

His experiences as an educator in tough urban communities shaped his belief in the need for holistic efforts to address the erosion of inner-city neighborhoods. Dr. Flowers's leadership led to the establishment of curriculum for St. Philip's which emphasizes academic excellence, a positive self-image and a faith-based focus for life. Alongside the strong academic program is a multi-faceted community center offering a wealth of social services and community development activities which are crucial to the revitalization of the surrounding neighborhood in which St. Philip's resides. This broad-based approach has established St. Philip's as a model for inner-city schools.

The St. Philip's Creed, which instills the limitless potential of children and youth, was written by Dr. Flowers in 1984.

Photo Credit: Tia Starghill

www.ingramcontent.com/pod-product-compliance
Lightning Source LLC
Chambersburg PA
CBHW041007170626
46815CB00002B/205